First Little Readers™

Fran Will Fix It!

by Liza Charlesworth

ISBN: 978-1-338-29799-7

Illustrated by Tammie Lyon

First printing, June 2018.

Meet a magic fairy named Fran.
She uses her wand
to fix things.

This girl needs a fancy dress.
"I can fix that," says Fran.

Fran waves her wand.
She makes the girl a fancy dress.
Oh, yes!

This frog wants to be a prince.
"I can fix that," says Fran.

Fran waves her wand.
Then she drops it.
Oh, no!

Look!
The wand is bent.
Will it still work?

Fran waves her wand.
She turns the frog
into a poodle.
Oh, no!

Fran waves her wand again.
She turns the poodle
into a puddle.
Oh, no!

Fran waves her wand again.
She turns the puddle
into a pickle.
Oh, no!

"What will I do?" cries Fran.
"I can fix your wand," says the pickle.
You see, the pickle was magic, too.

The pickle waves his wand.
He makes Fran's wand
as good as new.
Oh, yes!

"Thank you!" cries Fran.
"Now, what can I do for you?"
"How about you turn me
into a prince," says the pickle.

"Okay!" says Fran.
She waves her wand.
She turns the pickle
into a prince.
Oh, yes!

Then the prince marries
the girl in the fancy dress.
Oh, yes!

Then Fran makes them
a great big castle to live in.
Oh, yes!